THE TALKING YAM

adapted by Cheyenne Randall
illustrated by Cyndy Patrick

HOUGHTON MIFFLIN COMPANY

BOSTON

ATLANTA   DALLAS   GENEVA, ILLINOIS   PALO ALTO   PRINCETON

2

A long time ago, a farmer
was working in his garden.
He dug up a nice, fat yam.

"This yam will make a nice dinner,"
said the farmer.
"Put me down! Put me down!" said the yam.
"I want to stay in the dirt.
I don't want to be your dinner."

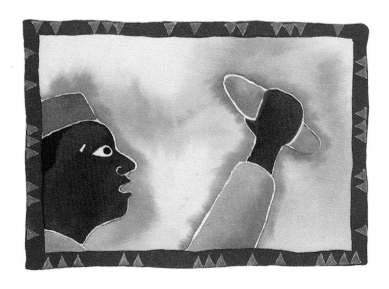

4

Now, everybody knows yams can't talk.
The farmer didn't know what to do.
He ran off to tell the king.

On the way, he met a woman and her goat.
"Stop! Stop!" said the woman.
"Why are you running like that?"

"There's a talking yam in my garden!"
said the farmer.
"It said, 'Put me down!'"
"Well, did you put it down?" asked the goat.

Now, everybody knows goats can't talk.
The woman and the farmer
didn't know what to do.
They ran off to tell the king.

On the way, they met a man.
He was cutting down trees with an ax.
"Stop! Stop!" said the man.
"Why are you running like that?"

"There's a talking yam in my garden!"
said the farmer.
"It said, 'Put me down!'"
"My goat talked, too!" said the woman.
"Well, what did the goat say?" asked the ax.

Now, everybody knows an ax can't talk.
The man, the woman, and the farmer
didn't know what to do.
They ran off to tell the king.

"Stop! Stop!" said the king.
"Why are you running like that?"

"There's a talking yam in my garden!"
said the farmer.
"My goat talked, too!" said the woman.
"So did my ax!" said the man.

The king frowned.
"Go home, all of you," he said.
"And stop telling such silly stories or
I will get angry."

YAMS
for sale

Kola
Nuts

14

The man, the woman, and the
farmer had to do what the king said.
They went back home.

The king sat down on his throne
and shook his head.
"A talking yam!" he said.
"That's just silly!"

"Yes, it is silly, isn't it?" said the king's throne. "Everybody knows yams can't talk."